KNIGHTS

vs.

DINOSAURS

HELAN

KNIGHTS

vs.

DINOSAURS

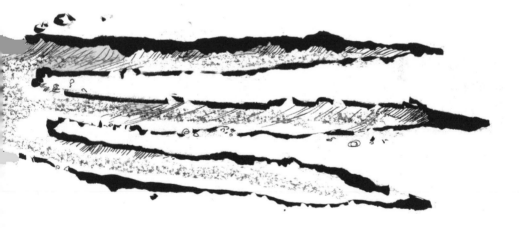

GREENWILLOW BOOKS
An Imprint of HarperCollins*Publishers*

Knights vs. Dinosaurs
Text and illustrations copyright © 2018 by Matt Phelan
All rights reserved. No part of this book may be used or reproduced in any manner whatsoever without written permission except in the case of brief quotations embodied in critical articles and reviews. Printed in the United States of America. For information address HarperCollins Children's Books, a division of HarperCollins Publishers, 195 Broadway, New York, NY 10007. www.harpercollinschildrens.com

The text of this book is set in Iowan Old Style.
Book design by Sylvie Le Floc'h

Library of Congress Cataloging-in-Publication Data is available.
ISBN 978-0-06-268623-7 (hardcover)
18 19 20 21 22 PC/LSCH 10 9 8 7 6 5 4 3 2 1
First Edition

Greenwillow Books

FOR JASPER

CONTENTS

KNIGHTS
VS.
DINOSAURS

CHAPTER ONE

A SLIGHT EXAGGERATION

When Sir Erec thought the whole thing over, he supposed that he shouldn't have said he'd slain *forty* dragons. Four might have been more realistic. He also shouldn't have boasted in front of Merlin, the one person in court smart enough to know that fierce dragons were—more or less—a flagon of hooey.

Now was not the time for reflection, however. A giant rampaging lizard had just tossed Sir Bors into a tree and was bearing down on poor Sir Hector.

Lance time, thought Sir Erec.

But perhaps it would be best to start at the beginning.

The banquet dragged on and on. Tales had been told, fruit had been juggled, songs had been sung (oh, so many songs). But the worst of it was Sharing Time. Each knight who had stumbled back into Camelot over the past few days now stood before King Arthur with a report of his adventures. Sir Erec thought it might never end.

Lancelot, naturally, had performed the bravest deeds; Galahad, the most noble. The rest scrambled for attention with various feats of derring-do, most of which were exaggerated, to say the least.

The knights all shared a deep secret. With the realm at peace, the knights spent a good deal of their time off in a field somewhere fighting *one another*. Not to slay, just for the sheer fun of it. They had armor and weapons after all. It was a shame not to use them.

Dragons, giants, trolls, and mythical beasts were in short supply. All knights believed in them without question, of course, but the pesky creatures couldn't exactly be counted on to make an appearance. Ever.

So the knights embellished. One tale after another of

battles with beasties, run-ins with rogue trolls, or fisticuffs with fierce giants.

Erec sighed. He was tired. His tunic was slightly scratchy. Whatever the reason, when it was his turn to share, out it came in a loud, clear voice. A whopping big embellishment to shame the rest.

"Did you say *forty* dragons?" asked Merlin with an air of polite interest.

"Yes," declared Sir Erec.

The Round Table exploded with excitement. Knights spouted support or disbelief or a combination of both.

All but the Black Knight. If you needed a tall, dangerously silent type, he was your man. No one had ever heard a peep from the Black Knight. Tonight, as always, he stood in a dark corner in full armor. He stayed rigid, staring at Erec through his visor and helm.

Queen Guinevere spoke, instantly silencing the hall.

"That is a most amazing accomplishment, Sir Knight. Have you no trophy for your king?" she asked.

Oh, dear, thought Erec. "Um," he began. "You see, milady, it was quite dark in the cave and—"

"The cave?" Merlin interrupted. "Where is this cave?"

"Far. Pretty far away actually."

"Oh," said Merlin, folding his napkin. "It is not the cave I am thinking of. Surely you would have not been so fortunate in that particular cave."

It was subtle, but the famous Merlin bait hung in the air. Merlin nibbled a carrot, waiting.

"Of what cave do you speak?" demanded Erec. He had no choice, really. This was all part of the act. If a dangerous adventure was dangled in front of you, a knight must respond.

Merlin cleared his throat.

"Oh, you don't want to know. For in this cave lives the

most fearsome creature of all: The Terrible Lizard."

"Lizard, eh?" said Erec. "I shall go and slay this Terrible Lizard!"

Sir Bors slammed a fist onto the table. "Nay! I shall slay it! Leave brave Sir Erec to rest after such a *noble* feat of slaying *forty* dragons."

The fever spread. Knights were a competitive bunch.

"I, too, should like to best this heretofore unknown creature!" piped Sir Hector, who had an interest in new and exciting beasts.

The Black Knight stepped forward. A hush fell over the room. A creaky nod of his helmet announced he would also join the fun.

Sir Erec rose and turned to King Arthur.

"My liege, with your permission, I shall face this Terrible Lizard." Erec looked back at Bors, Hector, and the Black Knight. "With these three coming along, I suppose."

Arthur poked at a stray pea on his plate. He often tuned out when the knights became overly excited.

"As you wish, brave knights. Mind the people, though."

"Of course, sire! Only the fearsome brute."

"Brutes," corrected Merlin. "There may be a few, come to think of it."

"The more the merrier," quipped Sir Bors. He was not exactly funny, but he often came up with a witty line at a crucial or dangerous moment.

Sir Erec gazed longingly at his mutton. But the deed was done. He had to make a show of it.

"I am off to prepare. I shall leave at first light."

"You will have the cave's location at dawn," said Merlin. "Bring no horses or squires into the cave. You may of course pack a weapon or two. Your choice." He smiled. His gray eyes sparkled.

"Splendid," said Sir Erec, but it came out less booming than he had hoped. The weekend was off to a poor start.

CHAPTER TWO

ADVENTURE, MERLIN STYLE

As the sun rose, Sir Erec perused the directions to the cave, which had appeared at his bedside. He then donned his armor with help from his squire, Derek. It took some time. Derek was more enthusiastic than he was skilled. For this reason Sir Erec usually left his squire at home when he went adventuring. Following Merlin's rule about not bringing a squire into the cave would not be an issue.

After a great deal of clanging, strapping, and adjusting, Erec was ready. Carrying his favorite broadsword and

shield, he clanked his way to the stables.
Sir Hector was already there, looking
quite trim and rested. His garments
were always rather clean despite his
numerous claims of adventures. Still,
Hector, aside from suspicious cleanliness, was not a bad
fellow. It could have been worse.

Then there was Bors. He was worse. A brute in shining
armor, Bors was a Might Makes Right man through and
through. Might Makes Right was the

philosophy that if you could
pound something harder than
the next person, then you
should do as you please. King
Arthur had been doing his
best to dissuade his knights of
this idea, but old habits die hard.

Bors's squire, a thin lad named Mel, struggled with the
knight's many weapons. He carried swords of all sizes, a
mace, a bludgeon, a lance, a shield, several knives, and

even a few rocks. Bors believed in being prepared for any and all encounters.

"Sir Erec!" bellowed Bors. "A fine day to smite a treacherous lizard, eh?"

"*Terrible* lizard, Bors," said Erec. "Get the name right. You don't want to confuse the minstrels later. Also, remember that my name is spelled with two *E*'s. The minstrels will need to know that as well, since I shall be the slayer."

"And you will not be alive to spell it yourself, I wager!" countered Bors.

Hector chuckled. "Good one, Bors!"

Erec simmered.

"It is very early in the morning," he said. "I will furnish a retort in fine wit momentarily."

THUNK!

A great ax chopped through a block of wood, startling the knights, the horses, and several chickens.

The Black Knight lifted the ax and regarded the knights. He turned and swept onto his midnight-black steed.

"Of course a witty retort is not always necessary," mumbled Erec.

"*Mel!*" barked Bors. "Load the weapons horse and follow me."

"Sir Bors, we are to leave our squires," said Hector.

"My squire is required as far as the cave. He will then tend to our horses. Did none of you think of that?"

Erec and Hector looked at each other. They shrugged, their armor creaking slightly.

"Looks like I'll be doing the thinking for this adventure," said Bors.

"Marvelous. This is getting better and better," Erec grumbled to Hector.

Erec snapped his reins and led the others to the gate. Hector followed, trying to jockey to the front. Bors took his horse to the left in an attempt to pass them both.

The Black Knight rode silently and steadily behind them with nothing to prove whatsoever.

"Yonder is the cave," announced Hector, pointing to a shale hillock with a small opening near the crest.

"Is that not the cave of Reginald the Hermit?" asked Bors.

"No," replied Hector. "Reginald the Hermit moved last summer. He wanted something with a nice view by a lake."

"Silence," commanded Erec. "We shall leave the horses here and proceed on foot. We know not the manner of this beast and must approach with caution."

"You would know, oh, great dragon slayer." Bors snickered. "I will approach on foot, but not because you suggested it. I thought of that moments ago."

"I, too, had created a similar strategy," piped Hector.

The Black Knight dismounted in silence.

The cave entrance was unremarkable. It was just wide enough for the four knights to enter single file, as they did in the following order: Sir Erec, the Black Knight, Sir Hector, and Sir Bors.

CLANG!

Oh, and Mel, Sir Bors's squire.

Mel carried a large, bulky canvas sack filled with weapons. It was the lance that gave him trouble at the entrance.

Erec looked back, annoyed.

"Bors, Merlin said no squires."

"Who will carry my weapons, then? I for one prefer to be prepared. Also, I have difficulty choosing sometimes."

"But Merlin—" Hector began to speak.

"Oh, Merlin! All talk that one with his rules and little tests. You never see Merlin slaying a dragon, do you? What does he know about anything?"

As if in answer, four torches suddenly ignited, lighting a passage deeper into the cave.

"Let's continue on," Erec said. He pulled his sword from its scabbard.

They followed the path and emerged in a small chamber of solid rock also lit by torches. A flat stone sat in the center of the chamber. On it was a large leather-bound book.

"This, uh, seems to be the end of the cave," said Erec, poking the wall with his sword.

"Perhaps the Terrible Lizard stepped out for a bite," said Hector.

"Well, it left its book," said Erec, poking the book with his sword.

"It can read?" asked Hector.

"*I* can't even read, you dunderhead!" snapped Bors.

"Who are you calling a dunderhead?" demanded

Hector. "I can read beautifully. My father believed a knight should be well rounded."

Hector inspected the book.

"It has a title: *The Terrible Lizards.*"

"Merlin sent us to slay a book?" growled Bors.

Hector opened the book. A strong wind blew through the cave and extinguished the torches.

Darkness. Silence.

"Well, it certainly seems to be Merlin's book," observed Erec.

A tentative voice came from the entrance to the chamber.

"Sirs?"

"What is it, squire?" barked Bors.

"Only that . . . you see . . . there's a tree outside the cave."

"So?"

"Well . . . it wasn't there before."

The Black Knight strode back down the passage. The other knights followed. At the mouth of the cave they stood stock-still for a moment. Then the Black Knight drew his enormous broadsword from its scabbard.

Directly outside the cave were the tops of tall vine-covered trees. Below spread a lush forest, overgrown with large ferns and moss. To the west, a barren land of dirt and dust and enormous rock formations.

"Merlin," said Erec.

"Merlin," gulped Hector.

"Merlin!" growled Bors.

The Black Knight pointed to the book in Hector's hands.

"Yes. Right," Hector said. "Perhaps there is some guidance here." He began to page through the book.

Erec gazed at the unfamiliar terrain.

"It must be an illusion. See if it says how to break the spell."

"'*Ty-ran-no-saurus rex*,'" read Hector slowly.

"Rex?" Erec interrupted. "That means king. A *tyrant* king. Splendid. It's a mission. We take care of this tyrant king and the illusion fades. Let's go."

"*Erm . . .*," muttered Hector.

"Close the book, Hector. Look lively," said Bors.

Hector closed the book. But he did not look particularly lively.

CHAPTER THREE

TERRIBLE LIZARDS

The entire landscape had changed. Behind them the cave itself was the same, but the shale hillock was now much steeper and surrounded by more rocky hills. As the knights descended, they entered a forest unlike any they had ever seen. Actually it resembled *all* the forests they'd ever seen trying to occupy the same space. It was not an orderly English wood.

"Where are the horses?" exclaimed Hector.

"The horses? Where is Camelot? Where is *England*?"

Erec's voice rose with each inquiry.

"Trickery and illusion," declared Bors. "Mel, my sword. You all wish you brought *your* squires into the cave now, eh?"

Mel reached into the canvas sack and fetched a fine sword.

"I shall explore the perimeter." Bors shut his visor. "Fear me, all who dwell h—"

Bors did not have a chance to finish his bellow. A tremendous creature burst from the trees and snatched

him up in its mighty jaws. The beast lifted Bors twenty feet off the ground and shook him like a puppy's chew toy. Fortunately Bors's armor held.

Sir Erec had seen some surprising things in his day. He'd been ambushed a time or two by barbarians hiding in trees. The Lady of the Lake had waved to him on one occasion. But nothing compared with what he now witnessed. This creature—calling it a lizard was a bit of a stretch although it was clearly reptilian—had a ridge of spikes that ran along its neck and back. It stood on two legs with nasty-looking claws at the end of its long arms. Its jaws held rows of teeth unlike any Erec had ever seen. They crunched into Bors's armor, denting deeper and deeper with each angry chomp.

Bors shouted from within the massive monster's jaws, kicking furiously.

The Black Knight was the first to remember that they were trained knights and leaped into the fray. A broadsword to the lower leg made the creature toss Bors aside.

Sir Erec swung his sword high and aimed for the tail, but the monster was fast for its size. The tail whipped around. Erec attempted to duck, but unfortunately a knight in armor is not the swiftest fighter. Sturdy, yes. Swift, no.

One swat from the tail sent Erec into the air. He landed on Bors.

"Get off me, Sir Knight!" barked Bors. "My honor has been . . . dented!"

Erec rolled over and took in the scene. Hector was off to the side, frantically paging through Merlin's book.

"Hector, what are you doing? Drop that book and engage!" yelled Erec.

The Black Knight had been cornered. The creature snapped its jaws.

"Ah! Here, beast!" Bors hollered, scrambling to his feet.

The monster spun, sprang into the air, and landed a few feet in front of Bors and Erec.

Hector placed the book safely by a rock, drew his

sword, and attacked from behind.

"Mind the fiery breath!" he shouted.

"It doesn't *need* fire!" countered Erec.

The Black Knight jumped in and stabbed at the monster's leg. It roared and swung around wildly, its thick, scaly tail sweeping across the area and easily knocking all four brave knights over like so many bowling pins.

They toppled through a thick brush and over a hidden precipice. One by one they tumbled down into a ravine below with a great deal of . . .

CLANG!

    CLANG!

        CLANGING!

The Terrible Lizard roared from the top of the slope. It looked, it sniffed, it tried a toe over the edge of the ravine, but then it thought better of the idea. With one final thrash of its tail, it was gone.

The battle had taken scarcely five minutes, but the knights' armor was more dented and scraped than it had been in the past five years of derring-do.

"What in Lancelot's name was that?" yelled Bors.

"Definitely *not* a dragon." Erec rose shakily and removed his helmet.

"Clearly not," said Bors. "In all my years I've seen one—well, obviously *several*—dragons but none that size."

"Or shape," said Hector.

"Or temperament," added Erec.

Mel slid down the hill dragging the sack of weaponry and holding Merlin's book.

Hector perked up. "Well done, squire! The book might—"

"Hang the book, Hector!" Erec said, wiping his sword with his tunic. "It's pretty clear. We have our Terrible Lizard to slay. Then we find this tyrant king fellow, make him bow to Arthur, and end this wretched spell! We don't need to read about it."

"Agreed," said Bors. "And the sooner the better. Squire! I'm in need of a bandage for my arm."

Mel looked stricken.

"I did not bring our supplies, Sir Bors. Only the weapons."

"No matter. Tear me a bandage from your tunic. In addition to this land looking entirely different, we seem to be experiencing the summer months. You will be fine."

"Perhaps one of these fronds or leaves would do better. They are quite sizable, my lord."

"I don't want a leaf!"

"I could find some herbs to go with it. A nice salve or natural ointment."

"I haven't got all day if you haven't noticed, boy! Your shirt! Bandage! Now!"

"No, my lord."

The knights all turned to stare at the squire.

"Did you say *no*?" Bors's complexion went from dark to torrential.

"I'm sorry, sir. I cannot."

Mel clutched his tunic as Bors straightened to his full, intimidating height.

"I'm . . . I'm a girl, Sir Bors."

It had been a strange day. All four knights would have admitted that. And yet this new revelation was in its way even more startling than the events of the last several minutes.

"You're a what now?" growled Bors.

"A female. A girl. A squire still! But a girl squire."

Bors strode over to Mel. She quivered but held her ground.

Bors looked at her for a long moment.

He opened his mouth to speak.

He closed it again.

Then Bors turned and walked over to a rock to sit down.

"That's just wonderful. England is gone. We are facing a monster of epic strength. There's a mysterious tyrant king. And now my squire is a girl. Great. Fantastic.

Anyone else here a *girl?*"

The question was meant to be rhetorical.

But the Black Knight raised a hand.

CHAPTER FOUR

MORE TERRIBLE LIZARDS

The Black Knight stood without a helmet for the first time in anyone's memory. And it was true. The Black Knight was indeed a woman.

The others remained as silent and still as stone. No one so much as blinked.

The Black Knight spoke in a calm, measured tone. "My name is Magdalena. I am the daughter of Robert the Blacksmith. I have wielded a smith's hammer since the age of two. I've swung a sword since age four. I have kept my identity a secret not out of fear or shame. I simply did not wish to deal with the stupidity of other knights."

She drew her sword slowly.

"But now we are no longer in our Age, and we are most likely to die battling this infernal beast. Not that I mind that part. But I see no point in keeping up the ruse of my identity for you lot. So if anyone has a problem, let us discuss it with our weapons."

Still, no one moved.

Eventually Erec found his tongue.

"I think—I think we're all—I mean, *I* don't need to fight you. Personally. Anyone else?"

"No! No!" chirped Hector.

Bors eyed the Black Knight. She towered over him, her sword ready.

"I have other fights to fight," muttered Bors.

"Let's move on then, shall we? We still have a tyrant king to find," said Erec, getting to his feet.

The knights marched into the woods. Bors led the way without a look back at the others. Mel heaved the sack of weapons and followed, glancing back at the Black Knight in awe. Helmet on but visor raised, Magdalena brought up the rear.

They walked in silence except for the unavoidable creaking and clanking of armor. Erec felt slightly dizzy. Whether it was due to the battle with the lizard, the tumble down the hill, the fact that he hadn't had much to eat that day, or that he now found himself in the company of two people of the female persuasion, he could not say. It was a potent mix; that was for sure.

After a few minutes the knights entered a large clearing. There were strange, enormous flowers. There were buzzing insects (also strange and enormous). There was grass.

And there were several giant beasts grazing on the grass in the distance.

Bors raised his sword.

"Wait," whispered Hector.

The creatures continued to graze. A few lifted their heads to regard the knights with mild interest.

"They appear to be docile," continued Hector. "Like a herd of cows."

"Monstrously sized cows," added Erec.

"How many kinds of terrible lizards are there?" asked Bors.

"A bookful, it seems," said Erec.

Smiling, Hector turned to face the company.

"But not all bad! You see? Just very large cows!"

One of the "cows" snorted. It lowered its head. Thick

horns protruded from its crown. It pawed the dirt. Others began to do the same.

"I think they might be *bulls*, Hector," said Erec, lowering his visor.

"Hmm?" Hector still had his back to the beasts. He looked over his shoulder just as the creatures burst into a stampede that shook the ground.

"Ah! Attacking cows! Attacking cows!" screamed Hector, fumbling for his sword.

Mel ducked behind a boulder as the herd came thundering toward them. They made an uncanny, high-pitched screech. It was no moo.

The knights scattered. Erec was knocked aside. Bors tripped over Erec's leg. His sword flew straight up, then came back down. Bors, eyes bulging, shifted just as the sword struck the ground an inch from his cheek.

Hector, blinded in a cloud of dust, swung his sword wildly.

The Black Knight had managed to wrestle one of the creatures to the ground and was pulling hard on its horns. It let out an ear-piercing shriek.

And a deep, rumbling bellow answered from the nearby woods. Birds took flight. Even the bulls paused.

"That does not sound good," said Erec.

The tree line exploded. Trunks crashed to the ground. An enormous monster rammed its way through. Its head was attached to a long, long neck of sheer muscle. Its tail whipped and took down three trees. The roar was deafening. The behemoth's front legs came crashing down like sledgehammers.

The bulls turned away from the pesky knights to face this more serious opponent. They charged at the giant.

"Retreat!" shouted Erec.

The Black Knight grabbed Mel and pushed her along.

The knights made for the trees. A pack of the spiky-spined terrible lizards burst onto the scene directly in front of them.

"Other way!" yelled Hector, tripping over Bors, who clanged into Erec, who slammed into the Black Knight.

The lizards sniffed the air. Unimpressed by the bumbling

knights, they joined the ongoing mayhem, fighting both behemoth and monster bulls with apparent glee.

The knights and Mel took the opportunity to run as fast as they could, not daring to stop until they were deep into the cover of the woods.

Safe. For the moment.

CHAPTER FIVE

TERRIBLE KNIGHTS

ONK!

Bors's armored fist came down on Sir Erec's helmet.

"What was that for?"

"Getting in my way!"

"*Your* way? You were in my way, you oaf!"

"*Oaf?*"

"Do you prefer *lummox?*"

Bors shoved Erec. Erec shoved Bors.

Hector tried to break it up and was kicked in the

shin for his effort. So he kicked back instead.

They pushed. They slapped. They fell over. It was clanging and awkward.

"If I were alone, I would have smited all of the creatures with ease!" said Bors.

"Smote," corrected Hector.

"Watch it, bookworm," Bors said, turning to Hector.

"You think you'd be better alone?" shouted Erec. "I know I would! I'm the king of alone! I adventure solo! No squire! No companions! No irritating, clumsy oafs to trip over!"

"Oaves," corrected Hector.

"*Oaves* is not a word. I can read, too, Hector," snapped Erec.

Magdalena sighed and sat on a fallen tree trunk. Mel dropped the sack of weapons. She looked at the Black Knight. Magdalena indicated the trunk with a wave of her hand. Mel joined her.

"Thank you, sir, um, ma'am," said Mel.

The Black Knight glanced at Mel and then spit a bit of blood onto the ground.

Bors swung out a leg and knocked over Erec.

"Might Makes Right!" shouted Bors.

"Why don't you Might Makes Right yourself out on your own, then?"

"I will indeed!" said Bors, slamming his visor shut. "You all are slowing me down. I'll have this tyrant king defeated by nightfall."

"I, too, shall go off alone!" chimed in Hector. "It will give me a chance to read Merlin's book, which might provide a clue to getting out of this mess. A fact that you knights are too dense to see."

"Reading a book is not going to help. But please feel free to find yourself a nice comfy spot somewhere," said Erec. "The rest of us will search for and deal with this king. Are we all agreed to venture on our own, then?"

They all turned to the Black Knight. The Black Knight had already left.

Bors yanked some weapons from his sack and stalked into the trees.

Hector, with the book strapped to his back, charged in a different direction, sword in hand.

Erec dusted off his armor. He glanced up. Mel was still sitting on the fallen tree. He looked around. They were alone.

"Splendid," Erec muttered. "Come along then."

He headed into the trees. Mel lifted her sack and set off after him.

CHAPTER SIX

TRICERA-JOUST

Sir Erec trudged through the woods with Mel trailing behind him. He stopped abruptly, unbuckled his leg armor, and tossed it aside.

Mel reached for the armor.

"Leave it. It's just slowing me down. Besides, you are *not* my squire," said Erec.

Mel nodded.

Erec continued at a faster pace. Mel tried to keep up.

Erec glanced back. Mel met his eye, then looked away quickly.

Erec sighed.

"So . . . have you always been a girl?"

"Yes, sir."

"Hmm."

They walked some more in awkward silence.

"What about your name? Is it truly Mel?"

"I shortened it from Melancholy."

"*Melancholy*. Cheerful."

"I *am* a good squire, sir."

They left the cover of the woods and entered a dusty clearing.

"I didn't want to be a scullery maid or a serf's wife or a—"

Erec held up a hand. He sniffed the air. He glanced around.

"It's not that I don't find your tale fascinating. And to be perfectly honest, I see your point. But I believe we are not alone."

"Yes, sir."

A brutish creature meandered into the clearing. It was sturdy and solidly built, standing a few feet taller than Erec and measuring the length of a large cart. It had a shieldlike crest over its eyes and three serious-looking horns protruding from its head. Each horn was the length of a sword.

The creature saw them and snorted. It squawked.
It took a few steps closer. It squawked more loudly. It
waited. Then it narrowed its eyes and lowered its head,
taking aim with its three horns.

"Squire—" said Erec.

Mel was already holding out a short lance.

"Excellent choice."

Erec moved into the clearing to face the brute. The beast eyed him but did not charge.

Erec stepped closer, lance raised and ready.

"I've seen worse than you. Wouldn't mind a good horse at the moment, but it can't be helped."

Erec got into position.

"Come now, terrible lizard with pointy weapons, what say you to a bit of sport?"

The creature charged. Erec charged. His lance hit the creature directly between the eyes. The beast grunted, veering off to the side.

"Ha! I wish Arthur could have seen that! Or better yet,

Guinevere." Erec grinned at Mel and winked.

Mel nodded and pointed. "Sir, I think you'd best—"

The beast circled back again. Erec snapped into action. This time the creature deflected Erec's lance and scooped him off the ground. It shook him once, twice, three times, then tossed him aside like a twig.

Erec landed with a thud. Dust swirled around him. When he raised himself to a sitting position, a knight-shaped imprint was left in the dirt behind him.

The three-horned monster squawked and charged from across the clearing.

Erec's lance had landed several yards away. Mel ran for it, but she would never reach it in time.

Erec looked around quickly. A few feet away was a fallen log about the size and length of himself. He dived toward it.

He planted his boots firmly on the ground. He put his shoulder into the log. It was heavy, but Erec put all his strength to the task. It lifted.

Erec held until the very moment the creature was upon him and then:

"Ha!" shouted Erec. He admired his work.

The log creaked under the weight. The beast growled.

Mel cleared her throat. "Sir, perhaps we should take advantage of this moment and—"

"Run?" asked Erec.

"Yes, sir."

"I concur."

They ran into the woods and soon found shelter behind some large rocks. They sat and caught their breaths.

After a moment Erec spoke.

"My squire is worthless, you know."

He looked at Mel and smiled.

"Bors is lucky to have you."

CHAPTER SEVEN

SIR HECTOR AND THE FEARSOME CHICKENS

Sir Hector had been trekking alone in the forest for some time without incident. He was uncomfortably warm but still in one piece.

When he came upon a secluded clearing with a nice inviting rock, it seemed perfect for a little sit-down.

He surveyed the entire clearing.

He poked the overgrowth with his sword.

It appeared to be lizard free.

Hector put his sword and shield down by the rock.

He unstrapped Merlin's book from his back, pausing a moment to admire the leather binding.

"I don't care what the others think. This book must be important. And I for one am going to read it."

He settled comfortably, opened the book, and began to read.

Hector turned the pages with a mixture of awe, horror, and excitement.

"Fascinating. Just fascinating," he muttered.

He read and read, flipping pages, going back and forth, making noises like "hmm" and "oooh" and "gadzooks."

"They are rather incredible, really. So much variety, too."

The bushes rustled.

Hector looked up.

A twig snapped.

He slowly reached for his sword.

A small creature hopped into the clearing. It was the size of a chicken. It even had feathers of many bright colors. But it also had the scaly head of a reptile.

Large, inquisitive eyes blinked at Hector. It tilted its head and chirped. For a terrible lizard, it was adorable.

"Hello!" said Hector gently.

The chicken took a step back.

"It's all right, my small friend. I won't harm you."

Hector put the book down and inched toward the shy creature.

"There, there. That's a good chicken. Don't be frightened of old Hector. I am a Knight of the Round Table."

Hector reached out slowly.

The chicken let him stroke its head gently. It almost seemed to be smiling.

"That's right. That's right, my little friend."

The chicken closed its eyes and made a little purring noise.

Then it locked its little jaws around Hector's finger, clamping down *hard* with a row of tiny razor-sharp teeth.

"Yowwww!"

He shook his hand, but the chicken would not let go.

Hector fell backward. He looked up in time to see another chicken sailing through the air, teeth bared, before it landed on his head.

"Eeee!"

Hector rolled over, swatting wildly. The two chickens jumped off and regrouped. The first chicken opened its cute little mouth and whistled shrilly.

Suddenly the bushes exploded with chickens. Hector was completely surrounded.

He looked about him uneasily. He lifted the book. For a long moment nothing moved.

And then the chickens snapped simultaneously into action.

"Ack!" Hector swung the book, knocking chickens into the air.

Even more appeared to take their place. Hector tripped

and was instantly set upon by the tiny, vicious cuties. They scratched, nibbled, and pecked the noble knight.

His opinion of the creatures soured considerably.

CHAPTER EIGHT

SIR BORS AND THE MACE-TAILED MENACE

Bors swung his sword with a fierce and mighty roar.

CRACK! CRACK!

The tree didn't stand a chance.

"Arrr!"

Bors kicked the tree for good measure.

He was frustrated. This was unusual. And bothersome. Bors liked to know where he stood. He had no patience for magic and spells. He had no tolerance for boy squires becoming girl squires. Or always being girl squires but tricking him. *Tricking* Sir Bors!

"*Arrrrrrrrr!*"

He smote the tree once more.

What he needed right now was a good old-fashioned brawl. He needed a terrible lizard.

As if in answer, a low bark sounded in the near distance.

Bors crashed through the overgrown ferns. Before him stood a four-legged creature. Built low to the ground. Strong legs. Small head. Heavily armored back.

It hissed at Bors.

"Oh, you want to have a go, eh? *Right!*"

The creature thundered up to him, turned sharply, and whomped Bors with its tail. The end of the tail was shaped like a large, rounded stone.

Bors reeled back but quickly recovered. He admired the tail.

"A mace man, eh? Fine!"

Bors reached for his belt. His trusty mace was still there.

Bors and the mace-tailed menace squared off.

They burst into action at the same moment, bludgeoning and punching, biting and kicking. A tremendous cloud of dust obscured the frenzy of action.

Bors swung, but the beast avoided the blow and cracked him again with its tail.

Bors pivoted and conked it on the head.

The creature grunted, shook its head, and plowed into Bors with its plated skull. Bors took it in the gut and fell backward onto his bottom.

He regarded the terrible lizard.

The terrible lizard regarded Bors.

It snorted.

Bors snorted.

Bors rose slowly and raised his mace. The creature raised its tail. And they went at it again.

The beast knocked Bors to the ground. It rose up on its hind legs to crash down, but Bors rolled out of the way and grabbed hold of the tail. The terrible lizard swung him to and fro but could not shake the brave knight.

"You—ah . . . *gah!*"

A cacophony of gut-wrenching roars and shrieks rang from beyond the clearing. Both Bors and the mace-tailed menace paused in midfight.

Trees toppled as five vicious, biting, extra-terrible lizards thrashed their way onto the scene. They tore and bit and kicked one another so intently that they didn't even notice Bors and his opponent.

The mace-tailed lizard charged into the fracas.

Bors watched.

He smiled.

"Wait for me! Huzzah!"

CHAPTER NINE

MIGHT MAKES RIGHT

Sir Erec's and Mel's respite had been short-lived. Currently they were racing through the forest at top speed.

"Don't look back! Don't look back! Don't look back!" called Erec.

They crashed through some thick foliage and tumbled down a steep hill.

Erec scrambled to his feet and peered back up the hill. Nothing. They'd escaped.

"All clear," he said, just as Hector burst out of the

bushes and collided with both Erec and Mel.

"Hector! What the—" Erec started to speak.

"Shh!" Hector was wild eyed and twisting back in the direction he'd come.

Three chicken-size lizards zipped out of the forest and perched on a rock.

They all stared at the creatures for a moment.

"You've got to be kidding, Hector."

The chickens bared their teeth and growled.

"They're rather worse than they look," whispered Hector.

A shield appeared, blocked the sun momentarily, and came down on the chickens from behind with a WHUMP.

The Black Knight lifted the dazed chickens off the rock and tossed them far into the woods.

"Thanks," said Hector.

She turned back to the knights. Her armor was scratched, dented, and muddied. Otherwise she looked just fine.

"Any, uh, trouble with terrible lizards out there on your own?" asked Erec.

"You should ask them," answered the Black Knight, wiping her sword clean.

The area was secure for the moment. Erec, Hector, and Magdalena rested in the shade. Mel organized the sack of weapons.

Hector opened the book.

"I've had a chance to peruse most of the book. It is absolutely fascinating. The illumination work is also quite accurate. I did not know that Merlin was such an artist."

"I have heard that Merlin has enchanted an owl to both write and draw," said Mel.

"Bah." Erec cut in. "Enchant an owl to draw?"

"He enchanted *us* to this wretched place. I should think he could manage to teach an owl to draw," said Magdalena.

"At any rate"—continued Hector—"these terrible lizards are extraordinary in all ways. They're not dragons exactly—"

"They're knights!"

It was Bors. He was standing at the edge of the clearing, bloody and wild eyed with excitement. It was not often that Bors's mind formulated an insight of any kind. He was on fire with the thrill of enlightenment.

"It's true!" He bounded up to the others.

"They fight us. They fight each other. They fight to conquer, to eat, and, I think, to have *fun*! They have armor, and their claws and teeth are as sharp and true as any blade. Knights! You see?"

"Knights?" said Erec dubiously.

"*Perfect* knights," asserted Bors.

"Whom do they serve?" asked the Black Knight.

"That's the best part." Bors chuckled. "They serve none but themselves. Might Makes Right. Proof in the pudding."

"Might Makes Right. Arthur says Might should be used only in service of the greater good," stated Erec. It was Arthur's guiding principle, and Erec agreed with him.

"Well, perhaps our king is misguided on that point," said Bors.

Mel drew her breath in sharply.

"How dare you." Hector stood.

"If you see Arthur, let me know. But in case you haven't noticed, Camelot is *not here*."

Bors stomped up to Hector and leaned into him face-to-face.

"We are knights. They are knights. We are

pitted against each other fairly. Together we show them who is stronger."

Bors leaned in closer.

"Might. Makes. Right."

Thunderous roars tore through the charged air. The group froze. The roars trailed off into dead silence.

"Where did that come from?" asked Erec.

"*Everywhere,*" said Mel quietly.

They drew their weapons silently. Each knight looked in a different direction. Mel crept behind a boulder.

"Maybe they're gone," said Hector.

Then a tree crashed down beside him, and all was thrown into chaos.

Terrible lizards of all shapes and sizes roared and gnashed teeth and chomped at one another. Great tails swung out. Enormous clawed feet pounded the ground.

And then they noticed the knights. That was when things really got started.

FLIP.

HMFF!

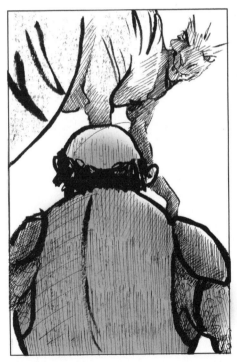

POW

The knights and Mel ran for their lives.

The ferns gave way to a rocky landscape. Hills of stone rose up everywhere. In a wall of solid rock there was one narrow crevice.

"In here!" shouted Erec.

The knights squeezed through the opening in single file. Sparks flew as their armor scraped against the rock walls. One spark lit the weapons sack on fire, but Mel immediately smothered it. At the opening of the crevice the terrible lizards screamed and roared and scraped claws against stone, but it was no use. They were too large to follow.

The crevice turned into a very long passage, and the knights shuffled through it. Eventually it opened up into a craterlike area surrounded on all sides by steep rock walls.

The crevice appeared to be the only entrance. In the center of the crater was a peaceful lake, shimmering in the late-afternoon sun.

"We'll be safe here. It's hot. I suggest we have a swim to restore ourselves," said Erec.

He glanced at the Black Knight and Mel.

"Er, undertunics *on*. I think we all can agree."

The knights did agree. It was the first thing they had agreed on all day.

Mel, who was not a strong swimmer, opted to sit by the water's edge and organize the armor and weapons. She laid them out against the rocks.

The others stripped to their underthings and waded into the water.

It felt really, really good.

CHAPTER TEN

A CALM,
COOL SWIM

The lake was large but not intimidatingly so. The knights floated, treaded water, and bobbed along contentedly.

Mel had cleaned the weapons and armor and set them in the sun to dry. She now paged through Merlin's book.

The knights, enjoying the quiet ripple of the lake, were silent.

"This reminds me of a pool near my home," said

Hector, finally. "I go there sometimes with my falcon."

"You are a falconer?" asked Bors. "So am I."

"Now a falcon is a predator I can get behind," said Erec, floating on his back.

"Their skill in hunting is quite admirable," said Magdalena.

"Strong claws," said Bors. "Could crush a man's hand. Well. Not mine, of course."

"They do have their whimsical side, too." Hector

chuckled. "They like shiny objects, just like ravens."

The conversation drifted into a pleasant silence.

"This is rather nice, fellow knights," said Erec. "Dare I say . . . peaceful?"

SPLASH!

The lake erupted beneath them as an enormous serpent broke the surface. Its neck was long. Its fins were massive. Its teeth were sharp. Life could certainly be unfair to the knights.

The serpent dived for Erec. Its neck swooped up before plunging down, teeth shining. But then it stopped in mid attack.

Bors was holding it by the neck.

The creature thrashed frantically. Its tail knocked Hector into the air, splashing him down a few yards away. He took a deep breath and swam underwater toward the belly of the beast.

The serpent reached back for Bors with its deadly jaws,

but the Black Knight burst out of the water beside it and grabbed its head.

Hector wrapped his arms around one flipper so it couldn't swim.

Erec climbed onto its back and pounded away with his fists.

The knights fought as one. There was no need for instruction. None swam to safety.

The serpent writhed with fury, knocking Bors, Hector, and Erec off.

But the Black Knight held tight, her grip like a steel vise, her focus singular and unshakable. The creature rolled, it leaped, it splashed, but nothing could shake the great knight.

Mel watched anxiously from the shore. Her mind raced. The weapons were too heavy for aquatic combat; besides, she'd never be able to throw a sword that far. But— *but*—

Mel grabbed a rock the size of her head.

At that very moment the Black Knight looked up.

Holding the serpent's neck with one arm, Magdalena lifted her other hand high.

Mel launched the rock with all of her might.

It sailed straight to Magdalena's hand, and in one smooth movement she brought it down on the serpent's head. The creature ceased its struggle instantly and sank below the surface, down to the depths.

The knights bobbed in the water, looking at one another.

They all nodded. It meant "nice work."

They began to swim to the shore.

Mel stood by the armor and weapons sack. The sun crept out from behind a cloud. The armor glistened brightly.

And that was when they heard the flapping sound.

Four gigantic flying lizards descended toward the shore in a flash. The knights swam faster, but it was no use. They watched helplessly as the flying creatures snatched the armor from the ground.

"Shiny . . . objects," sputtered Hector.

The flying lizards squawked and screeched. More came, each stealing away with the armor, the shields, the swords, the sack of weapons.

And Mel.

She struggled in the grip of the talons as she was carried up and away into the sky.

The knights reached shore and watched the flying lizards escape with everything except Merlin's book.

No one spoke.

Then Bors grabbed a large rock, gripping it in his massive fist until his knuckles were white. He started up the hill.

"Be he lad or lass," Bors growled, "no one steals *my* squire."

CHAPTER ELEVEN

SHINY OBJECTS

Mel had fainted. It was perhaps due to the height. Or maybe the ferocity and grip of the flying lizards. It could have been the sudden realization that all hope was lost. Any one of these things might cause a person to swoon. All combined? Fainting could hardly be helped.

She came to in an enormous nest made from hundreds of tree branches. A single flying lizard perched on a thick limb. The nest was so deep that when she stood, she was just able to see over the edge. But doing that was a mistake on two counts: one, it confirmed that the nest was perched on a very high mountain, and two, the flying lizard in the nest didn't seem to like her standing up without permission.

It screeched, and Mel's ears rang in pain. She sat back down. Beside her were various pieces of shining armor, swords, and the sack of extra weapons. Next to the sack was an enormous spotted egg.

Another flying lizard swooped down, its immense

wings generating a strong breeze. Mel flinched. The two fierce creatures stared at her. They blinked their beady eyes. But they did not attack. Mel was puzzled.

She looked at the egg beside her. She looked back at the flying lizards.

They looked at the egg and then looked at her.

Mel gulped.

She was baby's first meal.

Erec shaded his eyes as he stared up at the top of the mountain.

"That's the nest. I just saw her head poking out. She's still alive. But we'd better move fast."

He turned back. At the edge of some woods Bors, Hector, and Magdalena were pulling down thick, long vines.

"How's it coming?"

Bors tightened a knot of vines. He held up an end that had been looped into a lasso.

"It'll hold."

"Let's hope so, Sir Knight," said Erec. "Onward and upward."

Mel was trying to quiet the part of her brain that was filled with terrified screaming. She must think. She must find a way. This was the sort of thing she did. This was what she was good at. A squire was always thinking, planning, preparing.

Weapons. There are plenty of weapons, she thought.

One of the lizards hopped up suddenly. It landed again, perched close to the sack.

Okay, she thought. Perhaps not.

No! Be brave. She reached slowly for a sword.

The lizard snapped its beak and flapped its mighty wings.

Mel froze. Then she pulled back her hand and held it out to show that she was unfortunately without a weapon.

The knights ascended. They climbed steadily and in silence except for the occasional grunt. Erec took the lead. He tossed the lasso end of the vine up and around a jutting rock, secured it, and the others climbed up the makeshift rope after him. Then they repeated the process.

Climbing up to the next ledge, Bors reached for a crevice in the rock. He released his grip on the vine. The rock gave, and Bors fell.

His descent was short. Magdalena caught him with one powerful arm. She held the dangling Bors until he managed to grab hold of the vine once more.

He looked up at the Black Knight. He nodded.

She nodded.

They continued the ascent.

Mel wavered. She was feeling beaten. The flying lizards were too large. Too fast. Too attentive. It was hopeless.

But I mustn't give up, she thought. I have survived so far in this strange place. I have risked so much already, but—but—

Despair returned. *What* had she done exactly? Her days as a squire were over. She almost cried.

Almost.

But Melancholy Postlethwaite was made of sterner stuff. She would find a way. She just needed time.

At that moment the egg began to crack. A beak as long as Mel's arm poked through the shell. Mel looked up at the flying lizards. They were focused on her, their black eyes narrowing.

Finally the knights reached the ledge just below the nest. Magdalena coiled the long rope carefully and handed the lasso end to Erec.

"You throw it, Sir Erec. Your aim is best."

Erec took the vine.

Hector made room on the ledge for Bors to pass ahead of him.

"Sir Knight, you punch with far more accuracy than I. You go first."

"You are too kind, Sir Knight," said Bors.

Erec turned once more to his companions.

"Everyone know the plan?"

"Fight," said Hector.

"Get swords," said Magdalena.

"Then stab," said Bors.

"Splendid," said Erec.

The baby lizard broke free of the egg. The larger flying lizard spread its wings and shook them, readjusting its perch. The other opened its beak, revealing its razor teeth. It shrieked at Mel.

There was no time left. She inched her hand toward the nearest sword. Once she got it, she would fight with everything she had. She would not win, but she would die honorably. If only—

A lasso made of thick vine sailed over the side of the nest and landed beside her. Mel understood in an instant and quickly secured the rope to a large branch in the nest.

The lizards shifted and screamed. And then four Knights of the Round Table climbed onto the edge of the nest.

The knights roared and attacked. The flying lizards

shrieked and flapped into action. In a flash Mel supplied the knights with swords.

The baby lizard screamed out with hunger. Mel knew that the adult lizards would fight without mercy to protect their young. They needed an escape plan fast.

She found one. The vine!

Mel loosened the vine and pulled up the slack. She quickly threaded it through some helmets and armored breastplates. She secured the sack next, then attached the shields. She made a second lasso at the end of the vine.

Hector fought back one of the lizards. He checked on Mel and saw what she had done with the vine. The plan clicked. He grabbed one end of the rope.

Mel lassoed her end around the leg of the nearest flying lizard as it flapped its wings and lifted up. Hector did the same with the other end, attaching it neatly to the leg of the second flying lizard.

"Sir Knights!" shouted Mel. "Grab hold!"

The others joined Hector and Mel, gripping the vine. Soon enough the two flying lizards discovered that they were also attached to the strange rope. They were not amused. They rose higher in the air.

"Now!" shouted Erec.

The company, holding fast to the rope, leaped over the side of the nest. The flying lizards tried to escape, but they were connected by twenty feet of strong vine. More vexing still, the vine was weighted by armor, a sack of weapons, four knights, and their baby food.

The beasts flapped in vain, but they could only slow the descent. Down, down, down they glided.

As they neared the ground, Erec called out, "One. Two. Three!"

The knights let go of the vine and crashed safely into the dirt.

The Black Knight rolled and leaped up, sword held high. She sliced through the vine and the armor and sack slid off.

The furious creatures, free at last, rose swiftly. They screeched at their enemies but did not return.

The group all rose to their feet, dusting themselves off.

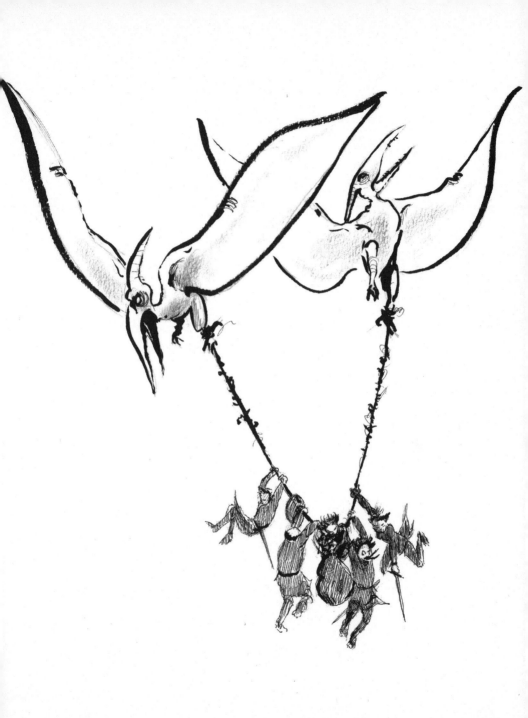

"Quick thinking, squire," said Erec. "I had frankly forgotten about an exit strategy."

"If there's one thing a squire knows, my lord," said Mel, "it's that armor and weaponry are rather heavy."

Hector and Magdalena patted Mel on the back and shoulder.

Bors nodded but said not a word.

CHAPTER TWELVE

COURT OF
THE REX

The company traveled on. During a rest Hector paged through Merlin's book and made an important discovery about who, or what, the *Tyrannosaurus rex* actually was. He took the opportunity to educate the others. They all examined Merlin's book.

"Crikey, he's a big fellow," said Erec. "Clearly the king."

"Yes, it would appear to be the most terrible of the lizards."

"Let's go meet him then," said Bors, gathering up his sword and shield.

They climbed steadily up an incline. The trees were smaller and more bare. The air was thick. The noises were fewer.

The Black Knight stopped.

"I think we are getting close," she said.

The others joined her and saw what had stopped her in her tracks.

The skeleton of a three-horned beast lay before

them. Its bones were picked clean.

"There's another," said Bors, pointing down the trail to the remains of one of the long-necked creatures. "It's massive. And apparently no match for the king."

Farther along were several more skeletons, some intact, some torn to pieces. The path was strewn with carnage.

Hector gulped.

"Steady on," said Erec.

They moved slowly past the hulking skeletons and carcasses. Insects buzzed, and small scavenger lizards rustled past occasionally. Otherwise all was silent.

The bone trail led to a wide, dusty valley. Rock walls climbed up the western edge, and canyons and hills lay to the north. To the east was a tangled mass of dead gnarled trees and dry brush. The entire place felt like death. Nothing could thrive here.

Nothing except the king.

The knights entered the arena cautiously.

Mel pointed and spoke.

"There, on top of that rock hill. That's our cave."

It was indeed the cave. Their trek had brought them back to where they had started. But the hill leading to the cave was on the far side of the valley.

Rooooooaaaaaarrrrrr!

From the shadows of the valley an enormous creature emerged and blocked the path to the cave. Its powerful muscles rippled with each step. Its tail swished slowly in the air. Sharp teeth, too long to be contained, protruded from its mouth. Despite its size, it moved fast and carried itself with poise and confidence.

"Right," said Bors. "Not so bad."

Rocks crumbled underfoot. Two more tyrannosaurs joined the first. Each was bigger than the last. Finally the largest and most fearsome *Tyrannosaurus rex* of all took its place at the lead.

Hector's mouth hung open slightly.

"Oh. My. Lancelot."

"Looks like we have the entire royal family to deal with," said Erec.

"One for each," said Bors.

"No," said Erec. "We fight together. Mel, go to the side there in the brush. Make your way toward the cave once the battle begins. Stay low and stay quiet."

"Sir, I am not leaving," said Mel.

Erec turned to face her.

"We fight *together*. You said so yourself." Mel stood her ground.

"Very well. Now would be a good time for you to come up with another exit strategy. Stay alive at least until you think of something," said Erec with a grin.

The tyrannosaurs sniffed the air, snorted, and twitched their mighty tails.

The knights turned to face the terrible lizards. They drew their swords.

"Fellow knights," said Erec, "I would like to make a confession. In truth, I did not slay forty dragons.

Furthermore, I have never in my entire life even seen a dragon."

There was silence.

"Neither have I," stated Bors.

"Nor I," said Hector.

"Not one," said Magdalena.

"But here, in this strange land, we have encountered the fiercest, most terrible creatures imaginable," Erec continued. "And time and again we, valiant knights, fought bravely and well. We have matched them in strength and courage, and we have bested them in strategy." He nodded to Mel.

Mel nodded back.

"I say this not as a boast. It is the truth. Our deeds have no need for embellishment or exaggeration." Erec paused. "I have no illusions about what we now face. These monsters may very well be the end of us. They are certainly worthy opponents."

The largest T-rex took a step toward the knights.

"But we are Knights of King Arthur's Round Table.

This is a glorious day, and I cannot imagine being among a better band of heroes."

Shields raised, swords at the ready, the four knights strode toward the terrible lizards.

The tyrannosaurs attacked in a flash. The shields were no match for the force of the initial impact, and the knights were knocked back.

Erec swung at the belly of one beast. His sword glanced off the thick hide but did not pierce it.

No one's swords could penetrate the terrible lizards' armor. Bors, mace in one hand, sword in the other, attacked in a fierce combination of blows and stabs.

But the teeth and jaws were the real danger. The lizards were fast and furious, and their chomps brutal and nonstop.

Erec was the first to find himself lifted several feet off the ground. His armor kept the teeth from puncturing his vital organs, but the pressure of the monster's bite was tremendous. He whacked the terrible lizard on the snout. And then he whacked again. And again.

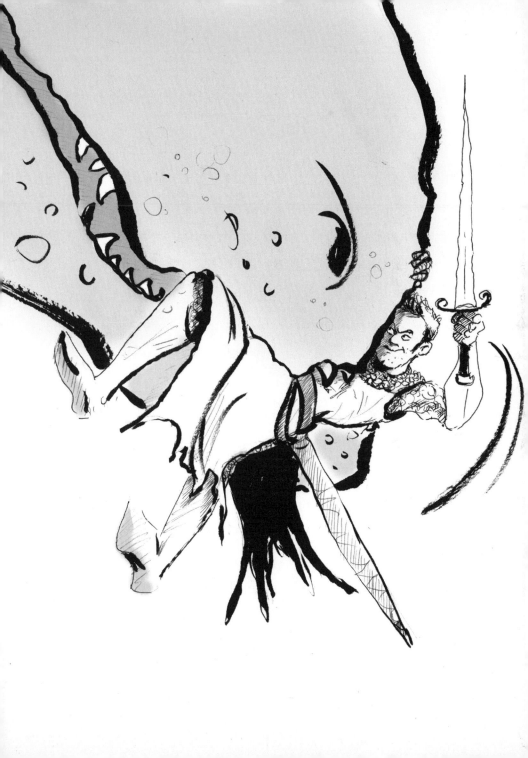

Sir Hector dodged the stomping legs of another tyrannosaur, pivoted, and brought his sword down on the tail of Erec's captor. The monster spun and loosened its grip enough for Erec to slip out and grab hold of its neck.

Its mercifully tiny arms reached and clawed, but to no avail. Erec kicked his leg against the beast's chest and flipped up onto its back. He gouged its eyes from behind.

Hector and Bors stood back-to-back, facing off against two opponents. The flurry of swords kept the beasts at bay but not deterred. They attacked with relentless energy.

When Erec was finally tossed from the bucking tyrannosaur, he landed harshly on the ground and rolled away just in time to avoid being squashed underfoot.

The Black Knight, sword in hand, fought back the largest of the tyrannosaurs. She saw Erec, badly winded with a T-rex ready to pounce on him. Erec struggled to his feet. His opponent snorted and slowly opened its jaws, saliva dripping to the ground.

Magdalena turned back to the gigantic T-rex and shoved a sword into its mouth, lodging the weapon in its jaws. As the monster struggled, she leaped onto its tremendous haunch and hoisted herself onto its back. She took a deep breath. And then, with amazing dexterity, she ran straight down the T-rex's spine, out onto the tail, and leaped off the monster just as the other T-rex launched itself at Erec.

The Black Knight landed between Erec and the beast. In a flash she lifted a discarded shield and blocked the creature. Erec got to his feet and threw a mace to the

Black Knight. Magdalena caught it and dealt the T-rex a mighty blow.

Mel watched in horror from the trees. The knights fought bravely—braver than any before surely—but the odds were against them. The tyrannosaurs did not stop. They would not stop.

She pulled the sack of extra weapons toward her. She might need to supply new weapons at a moment's notice—

Notice. Notice!

Her hand was gripping the bit of burned sack that had caught fire in the crevice by the lake. *Fire*. Mel dug into her pouch for her flint and striking stone. After several frantic moments a spark caught a dead tree branch. She blew the flame, and it rose and licked its way up the wood.

Mel waved the branch like a torch. Running along the edge of the arena, she spread the blaze. It wound through the dry brush to the hill where the cave was located.

"Sir Knights!" she yelled.

Those who could looked up. Unfortunately so did one of the terrible lizards. It roared in her direction. Then it charged. But Sir Bors launched himself into the air and brought his sword down on the monster's foot. It snarled and turned, teeth bared. Bors bared his own teeth and roared back. He swung one powerful fist in a precisely placed uppercut. The punch connected.

The terrible lizard's eyes crossed; it wobbled on its injured foot, then toppled over with a tremendous THUD.

Bors snorted and turned, fists ready.

"Go!" he yelled at Mel.

She ran, spreading the fire, which burned higher and higher.

Hector and Erec swung their swords at their foes,

knocking them back with each powerful blow. Soon Hector turned and ran toward the wall of flame. He bolted through a small opening in the blaze to join Mel. Erec came next, crashing through the fire. He stopped, dropped, and rolled on the ground to extinguish some stray flames.

Eventually Bors leaped through the fire to join the others at the foot of the hill. Three of the tyrannosaurs approached the line slowly, the inferno confusing and angering them. They roared. They chomped the fire, then recoiled in pain. The barrier was working.

"Where is the Black Knight?" said Mel, throwing her torch into the blaze.

The knights peered through the flames and smoke.

"There!" shouted Bors.

The Black Knight faced off with the tyrant king. They slowly circled each other. The king swished its tail and snarled. It snapped at her. She jumped away, landed, then attacked, bringing down her mace. The handle broke in two. Magdalena tossed it aside. There were no other weapons within reach. She ran for the fire line.

"Quickly!" called Erec.

The Black Knight stumbled and fell. The king was on her in an instant, snapping her up in its jaws, her armor creaking and groaning. She pushed at its upper jaw, but the powerful beast clamped down even harder.

That was when she got mad.

The Black Knight grabbed a single tooth and pulled and pulled and tore it right out of the king's gum. It opened its mouth in a roar of pain. The Black Knight took hold of the king's tongue, yanked it out, and swung to the ground.

Perhaps the king of the terrible lizards had never felt such a sensation. For a moment it didn't appear to know *what* to do, which was enough time for the Black Knight to race for the fire line again. She jumped straight through and landed safely on the other side.

The king stuck its enormous head through the flames, then pulled back with a roar. The terrible lizards panicked.

Smoke filled the clearing. As long as the fire around them raged, they were trapped.

"Ha-ha!" Erec chortled. "I'll bet they wish they were dragons *now*, eh?"

Bors slapped Erec heartily on the back.

"Good line, Sir Erec! Very witty indeed!"

And with that the company made a hasty climb up the hill to the cave.

CHAPTER THIRTEEN

THE END OF
THE ADVENTURE

With the fire keeping the *Tyrannosaurus rex* family at bay far below, the knights and Mel entered the cave and strode down the passageway to the book chamber.

"Hear us, Merlin!" said Erec in his most booming voice. "We have bested the tyrant king of the terrible lizards and herewith request our reward. Return us to England!"

A strong wind blew through the dark cave, then stopped suddenly.

Erec strode back to the entrance. He looked out.

"Ah, vermin! Didn't work."

A tremendous roar from somewhere below confirmed this to the rest of the company.

"Perhaps Merlin's book could help," Mel suggested.

Hector placed the book on the rock at the center of the chamber. He paged to the end.

"Oh, there appears to be a note. I shall read it aloud for you."

Hector cleared his throat. And then cleared his throat again.

"Oh, just read it already, Hector," said Bors.

Dear Knights,

I have detailed the aspects of the Terrible Lizards in these pages for your quiet perusal. However, it is likely you have ignored this volume entirely and ventured out to see for yourselves. I hope that worked out for you. And if there are any of you left and you still have heads, let alone eyes to read these words, I do hope you will reflect on your experience.

Terrible and magnificent creatures have indeed walked this earth. Perhaps they still do or will again one day. I hope that you now have a proper amount of respect for these fierce beasts and that this knowledge may help curb your more boastful assertions of knightly bravery and exploits.

And now my enchanted owl is tired and requests that I dictate no more for him to inscribe. Fare-thee-well or farewell, Brave Knights (whichever is the case).

Best,

Merlin

The knights looked at one another.

"Has this"—Erec began slowly and evenly—"has this

entire adventure just been one of Merlin's Teachable Moments?"

"Yes, I believe so," said Hector. "Furthermore, it appears that we could have simply sat here and *read the book*."

There was a long silence.

"Well, where would the fun be in that?" said Magdalena.

More silence.

Until a chuckle came from Bors. Soon Erec joined in. And Hector. And Mel. Magdalena smiled a rare smile, and then, even more extraordinary, she laughed.

The whole cave echoed with laughter.

And then four torches blazed.

The knights walked to the entrance and looked out.

"Merry ol' England," said Erec.

Indeed it was. There were fine trim oaks. The woods were orderly and proper. A squirrel hurried by. It wasn't even a large squirrel.

The knights descended the hill. They found their horses just as they had left them, grazing peacefully in the shade. The knights went to their steeds.

"One moment," said Bors, placing a hand gently on Mel's shoulder.

"Mel," he said. It was the first time he had ever used her name. "You have acted with cunning and bravery. Your contribution to this quest is undeniable."

Mel glowed. Warmth radiated through her. She stood a little taller.

"But—"

It was one small word. Yet her face looked as though Sir Bors had thrust a sword through her.

"I am afraid that I cannot have a girl as a squire. It just . . . it just isn't done."

He held out his hand. Mel knew what it meant, knew there was no argument to be made.

She handed Bors the sack of weapons that she had so dutifully carried.

He took it and secured it to the weapons horse. Then he mounted his own horse and set off, pulling the reins of the weapons horse behind him.

Erec and Hector each gazed at Mel silently, but then followed Bors on the path to Camelot.

Mel stood there alone. Small. Lost.

Until a shadow fell over her. She turned.

The Black Knight was beside her, high on her midnight steed.

"Come with me, if you like. Be whoever you wish to be." She lowered a hand. "A good squire is a good squire."

Mel smiled. She reached up, and the Black Knight easily lifted her onto the back of the horse.

They rode on without another word.

That evening the four knights returned to Camelot and the court of King Arthur.

They waited until all were assembled in the great hall. Especially Merlin. This entrance had to count.

The massive oak doors opened with a bit of tasteful fanfare. The Knights of the Round Table turned in unison.

Sir Erec, Sir Bors, Sir Hector, and the Black Knight strode in, still wearing their battle-scarred armor.

A hush fell over the hall.

Merlin sat up straight, a small inscrutable smile under his long beard.

"Approach," said Arthur.

Sir Erec strode before the king and queen and bowed.

"Sire, we have returned from battling the terrible

lizards. They were indeed fearsome, more so than any dragon in existence, but"—Erec looked back at his fellow knights—"*together* we bested them all."

"Step forward, all of you," said Arthur.

Hector and Bors approached and bowed. The Black Knight remained in the shadows, helmet and visor on as usual.

Arthur waited.

"All of you, I said." Arthur's voice was quiet, but that meant that he was really, really serious.

The Black Knight came forward. And for the first time in Camelot she removed her helmet. Magdalena bowed.

There were gasps. A few forks dropped out of the hands of stunned knights. Wine was spit out in surprise.

Arthur cleared his throat. Guinevere tilted her head slightly. Merlin merely nibbled on some lettuce. He didn't seem particularly surprised.

Erec broke the silence.

"Your Majesty, I know this is highly . . . irregular. But I must tell you and all here at court that before you stands the bravest and mightiest knight I have ever known.

"Sorry, Lancelot," Erec added quickly.

Lancelot waved it off. Little things didn't bother him.

"Your name?" asked Arthur.

"Magdalena, sire. Daughter of Robert the Blacksmith."

Arthur considered this for a moment.

"Very well, Black Knight."

Everyone exhaled.

"Join us for a feast, brave knights. Tell your tale. Teach the minstrels some new songs," said Arthur. "For all our sakes."

"Gladly, sire," said Erec. "But first—"

He glanced at Magdalena. She grinned. Magdalena

tossed something into the air, and Erec caught it without looking.

"My queen, we have brought a trophy for you and our king."

Erec held up an enormous tooth, a souvenir from the great *Tyrannosaurus rex*.

Guinevere took the tooth. Merlin's eyebrows rose with interest.

"Well, well done, brave Knights," said Guinevere. "A most terrible lizard indeed."

Erec bowed low.

The formalities completed, the hall once again filled with chatter, music, and excitement. Bors and Hector held various knights spellbound. Lancelot engaged in his first conversation with the Black Knight, who in truth, he had long admired. Even Mel was surrounded by the other squires in the antechamber of the great hall.

Minstrels were summoned, and they began to compose new and exciting songs.

Sir Erec, however, took his leave quietly and walked alone to the great door of the hall. His tunic was slightly scratchy. He was very tired.

The adventure was over, and his bed awaited.

CHAPTER FOURTEEN

BAND OF SIBLINGS

Erec slept deeply and soundly and free of dreams. He awoke to a breeze wafting into his bedchamber. A few songbirds twittered pleasantly nearby. He yawned. He was content.

Then the clatter of fallen armor rang through the outer rooms. After a timid knock the door opened a crack. Derek the squire poked his long nose into the chamber.

"Sir Erec?" he whispered.

"What is it, Derek? It had better be eggs and bacon."

"Um, not quite, my lord."

"Come in, squire."

The squire entered, holding a scroll of parchment.

"This arrived early this morning, Sir Erec, but I didn't want to wake you."

"Hand it here."

Derek did so and stood at attention.

Erec read silently. He rolled the parchment up.

He sighed.

"It seems," he said, getting out of bed, "that King Arthur has been so inspired by our magnificent adventure that he has proposed a new quest to all of the Knights of the Round Table."

He brushed Derek aside, grabbed some clothes, and swept through the door. Derek scurried after him.

"He wants us to search for the Holy Grail."

Erec put on his chain mail shirt and tunic.

"What on earth is the Holy Grail you may be wondering, my dear squire. Well, I'll tell you." He continued in a louder, slightly annoyed voice.

"It is a legendary item, lost for centuries, quite possibly not even in existence."

He fastened his belt and stepped into his boots.

"No clues, no leads. All of the earth to cover"—he threw open the front door—"in a search that is sure to be time-consuming and exceedingly dangerous."

There in the courtyard awaited Sir Hector, Sir Bors, and the Black Knight, all suited and ready, magnificent in their clawed and bitten armor and sitting on their finest horses. Mel was there, too, dressed smartly in black, riding a white horse behind the Black Knight. She held a new banner that showed a field of red with the silhouette of a terrible lizard at the center, surrounded by four swords. The same symbol decorated the shield of each knight.

"What an absolutely splendid idea." Sir Erec smiled.

A NOTE FROM MERLIN

Many of the terrible lizards (otherwise known as dinosaurs) in this tale did not truly walk the earth during the same eras or in the same regions. But didn't our heroes deserve the most epic battles? I thought that a more generous sampling of creatures from the ages might be more illuminating and entertaining for the knights.

Here are a few interesting facts about some of the dinosaurs in this book:

SPINOSAURUS

The Spinosaurus lived in the Cretaceous period, between 112 million and 97 million years ago. It was a carnivore, which means it ate meat. It had long spines forming a sail along its back. It was the biggest of all carnivorous dinosaurs and lived on both land and water, much like a modern-day crocodile.

TRICERATOPS

The Triceratops lived during the end of the Cretaceous period, about 68 million to 66 million years ago. It was an herbivore, which means it ate plants. The triceratops had three big horns on its skull and was about the size of an African elephant.

Ankylosaurus

The Ankylosaurus lived during the end of the Cretaceous period as well, about 70 million to 66 million years ago. It was an herbivore. It is known as one of the most heavily armored lizards because of the hard knobs and oval plates of bone that formed within its skin, such as what's found on crocodiles, armadillos, and modern lizards. It had a large club at the end of its tail thought to be used for self-defense.

Brachiosaurus

The Brachiosaurus lived during the late Jurassic to early Cretaceous periods, about 150 million to 130 million years ago. It was an herbivore. Its long neck allowed it to reach tall trees and vegetation not available to other animals. The Brachiosaurus could reach vegetation up to 39 feet off the ground and could eat up to 600 pounds of plant matter a day.

Elasmosaurus Platyurus

The Elasmosaurus platyurus lived during the Cretaceous period, about 80 million years ago. It was a carnivore. The Elasmosaurus platyurus was a marine reptile, with four long, paddle-like flippers that it used to swim slowly, similarly to turtles. It had a short tail, but a very long neck, with as many as 75 vertebrae in its neck alone.

Tyrannosaurus Rex

Tyrannosaurus rex lived during the late Cretaceous period, between 68 million and 66 million years ago. It was a carnivore, and ate mostly herbivorous dinosaurs. The Tyrannosaurus rex had a massive jaw and a strong bite—stronger than any other land animal that has ever lived. The largest Tyrannosaurus rex tooth ever recorded was twelve inches long.